THE FLOPSY BUNNIES

Based on the original story by
Beatrix Potter
with all new illustrations

Cover illustration by
Anita Nelson
Book illustrations by
Pat Schoonover

Publications International, Ltd.

When Benjamin Bunny grew up he married Flopsy, Peter Rabbit's sister. They had such a large family they were called the "Flopsy Bunnies." Because of so many mouths to feed, Benjamin used to borrow cabbages from Peter. But when Peter had no cabbages to spare, the Flopsy Bunnies went to the trash pile outside Mr. McGregor's garden.

The trash pile was a jumble of things, but one day—oh joy!—there was overgrown lettuce.

Benjamin and his children stuffed themselves with the lettuce leaves. Then they grew sleepy and lay down in the soft grass clippings. Benjamin slipped a paper bag over his head to keep the flies from bothering him.

The bunnies slept soundly in the warm sun. Far away, Mr. McGregor's lawn mower hummed. Flies buzzed, and a little old mouse named Thomasina Tittlemouse picked over the trash pile. She rustled across the paper bag and woke Benjamin Bunny.

While they were chatting away, Thomasina and Benjamin heard the steps of heavy boots. Just then, Mr. McGregor emptied a sackful of grass clippings right on top of the sleeping Flopsy Bunnies!

The little bunnies did not wake up in the shower of grass. But Mr. McGregor looked down and saw the tips of some furry little ears sticking up through the grass clippings. Then a fly settled on one of the ears. And the ear twitched.

Mr. McGregor climbed down onto the trash pile. "One, two, three, four, five, six little rabbits for supper!" he said, as he put the sleeping bunnies into his sack. The Flopsy Bunnies dreamed their mother was turning them over in their beds. They still did not wake up.

Mr. McGregor tied the top of the sack with string and put it on the edge of the garden wall. He left the sack sitting there while he went to put away his lawn mower.

While he was gone, Mrs. Flopsy Bunny came across the field. She looked at the sack sitting on the garden wall. She wondered where Benjamin and her children were.

While she was standing there trying to figure out what was going on, she heard a rustling noise off to the side. Thomasina Tittlemouse came out of the jar, where she had been hiding, and Benjamin took the paper bag from his head. They told Flopsy the sad tale.

Benjamin and Flopsy looked at the sack where their sleeping bunnies lay helpless. They took the sack down, but could not untie the string that bound it. What could be done? They had to come up with an idea soon.

Mrs. Tittlemouse was a very clever mouse. Thinking quickly, she began to nibble a hole in the bottom corner of the sack! The little bunnies were pulled out and awakened.

Benjamin and Flopsy then filled the sack with three rotten squashes, an old boot brush, and two overly ripe turnips. Then they all hid under a bush and watched for Mr. McGregor.

After a while, Mr. McGregor came back. He picked up the sack and carried it off. The Flopsy Bunnies followed at a safe distance. They watched him go into his house. They crept to the window to watch and listen.

The littlest Flopsy Bunny crawled up onto the windowsill to get a better look at what was happening. Mr. McGregor sat down at the table. The Flopsy Bunnies heard him chuckle, "One, two, three, four, five, six little rabbits!"

"Eh? What's that?" asked Mrs. McGregor. "What have the rabbits been spoiling now?"

"In the sack!" Mr. McGregor pointed to the lumpy sack on the table. "Six little rabbits for supper!"

Mrs. McGregor opened the sack. When she found the rotten vegetables inside, she was sure Mr. McGregor had tried to trick her! Mr. McGregor was angry, too. He threw a squash right out the window, and just missed the youngest bunny! It was time to go home, Benjamin decided.

That Christmas, the Flopsy Bunnies gave Thomasina Tittlemouse a very lovely gift—enough soft rabbit fur to make herself a coat, a muff, and a pair of warm mittens.